That Sky, That Rain

That Sky, That Rain

by Carolyn Otto • *illustrations by* Megan Lloyd

THOMAS Y. CROWELL • NEW YORK

Typography by Andrew Rhodes

1 2 3 4 5 6 7 8 9 10

First Edition

Library of Congress Cataloging-in-Publication Data
Otto, Carolyn.
   That sky, that rain / by Carolyn Otto ; illustrations by Megan
Lloyd.
      p.   cm.
   Summary: As a rainstorm approaches, a young girl and her
grandfather take the farm animals into the shelter of the barn and
then watch the rain begin.
   ISBN 0-690-04763-0 : $. — ISBN 0-690-04765-7 (lib. bdg.) :
$
   [1. Rain and rainfall—Fiction.   2. Farm life—Fiction.]
I. Lloyd, Megan, ill.   II. Title.
PZ7.O8794Th 1990   89-36582
[E]—dc20   CIP
                                                    AC

To Megan, and to my grandparents, Otto and Nicholson,
with deep down love.
—CBO

To Carolyn, of course, and to Tom, who saw the rain
when there was none.
—MLL

The artist wishes to thank Pete Kutulakis; Cary D'Alo Place;
and Dorothy Israel of Birdsong Gordon Setters.

Look at that sky.
We're in for some weather now.

Let's go, Sullivan. Lazybones.
It's going to pour any minute.

I always wanted a beard like that,
like old wire, wire and white paste.
Wouldn't your grandma just die?

Hold out your hands—both hands.
Whoa now. Talk soft now.
See there how her ears come up?

What a racket! What a fuss!
Sullivan, who asked you to sing?

This year I named them after my dinner—
Sweet Corn, Ambrosia, Okra, and Stew.
Stew? says your grandma. Ambrosia!
Next time, she says, I name the pigs.

Come on, Bessie. Come on now.
No sense waiting around for the rain.
Bessie and Bossie, Bossie and Bessie,
those are good names for cows.

Here she comes.

Stand here in the doorway and watch
how rain marks the edges of things—

the overhang of that white awning,

the space beneath the truck.

It's the most commonplace kind of magic,
clouds spilling down before your eyes.

You can open your mouth and drink
sky like a tall glass of water.

Look at that rain!